SAY HELLO AND LET IT GO
I AM NOT MY EMOTIONS

Written by: Jocelyn Soliz   Illustrated by: Kyle Fleming

SAY HELLO AND LET IT GO:
I AM NOT MY EMOTIONS

First Inspired and Rewired Publishing edition • May 2020

ISBN: 978-1-7346844-3-8 (paperback)
ISBN: 978-1-7346844-4-5 (hardcover)
ISBN: 978-1-7346844-5-2 (ebook)

INSPIRED AND REWIRED
PUBLISHING

This book is written for all of the children
who deserve tools to live happy and healthy lives.

Also, thank you to my family and friends
who have supported my mission to provide social
and emotional learning through books.

There is nothing wrong with any emotion you experience. You feel emotions every single day. Some emotions, like joy, make you smile from ear to ear. These emotions are so good for your heart and your brain.

There are other emotions, like anger, that make your body and brain do all sorts of interesting things. Sometimes, these emotions like to overstay their welcome.

The great news is that you get to decide when the emotion gets to take hold of your heart and mind.

You do this by noticing the visiting emotion, greeting it by name, letting it know you accept it, then sending it off on its way.

When you have a new toy, but no one wants to play . . .

Say hello, and let it go.

Hello, Sadness. I accept you.
I will see you another day.

When you wave "hi" to your friend,
but they turn and look away . . .

Say hello, and let it go.

Hi, Rejection. I will see you another time.
I am choosing to go on with my day.

When you ask for something, but you don't get your way . . .

Say hello, and let it go.

Hello, Anger. I see you, and I feel you trying to take control of my day.
You can go now. I will be on my way.

When you are told to clean before you can play . . .

Say hello, and let it go.

Hello, Irritation. I must be on my way now,
but I hope you have a great day!

When someone blames you for something you didn't do . . .

Say hello, and let it go.

Hello, Frustration.
Thank you for visiting.
See you later.

When you have exciting plans,
but suddenly they change . . .

Say hello, and let it go.

Hi, Annoyance. I see you. Goodbye.

When you trip and you fall with everyone watching . . .

Say hello, and let it go.

I see you there, Embarrassment.
Until we meet again...

When you get the painful news that someone you love has passed away . . .

Say hello, and let it go.

Hello, Devastation. I see you and feel you. I allow you to stay.
I just want you to know that when I am ready, I will send you on your way.

When you ask someone for help, but they turn you away . . .

Say hello, and let it go.

Welcome, Disappointment. I will see you another day.

When you have had an extremely bad day . . .

Say hello, and let it go.

There is no reason to run from these emotions or to let negative emotions ruin your day. Say hello to them, and then be on your way!

Author's Note

Are you looking for some tools to use when it isn't so easy to take control of your emotions? Try one of these three exercises when you feel your emotion may try to overstay its welcome.

Count backward from 10

Notice your emotion, call it out by name, now count with me. 10. 9. 8. 7. 6. 5. 4. 3. 2. 1. 0. If you are still having a hard time letting it go, count again.

Take three deep belly breaths

Notice your emotion and begin to focus on your breath. Place the palm of your hand on your belly, right on your belly button. Take a deep breath in through your nose and try to make your hand move away from your body with the movement of air entering your belly. Next, let out all of your air through your nose. If you want to try something fun, let your air out (exhale) through your mouth, curling your lips and pretending you are blowing through a straw. Repeat until you are ready to let the emotion go on its way.

Positive self-talk

Notice what emotion you are feeling. Say to yourself "I got this" or any other phrase that gives you confidence and courage to release your emotion. Some great phrases to use are:

- I'm amazing
- This is temporary
- Life is good

A Note to Caregivers and Teachers:

This book was written with mindfulness principles in mind. As simple as this book is, it will equip your little one with the tools they need to live with more peace and less suffering. I have broken down the principles used below.

Step 1: Noticing (Mindfulness)

When your little one takes the time to pause and notice an emotion, they are practicing mindfulness. With practice, pausing and becoming aware of emotions and sensations will become easier and more natural. The key here is that this skill takes time to strengthen. Pausing and noticing gives your child the ability to respond to their environment rather than reacting to it.

Step 2: Say Hello (Acceptance)

Mindfulness practices are not only about noticing emotions and thoughts. What you do next is just as important. We have a saying in mindfulness – "What you resist persists." So many of us spend our lives doing anything and everything we can to avoid uncomfortable sensations.

By "saying hello" to all emotions we are no longer running. We are changing our relationship with our emotions. There is no such thing as a "bad" emotion. If we don't like the way an emotion feels, we do not have to spend our lives avoiding it. We can acknowledge and accept the emotions as they come - because they will come.

Step 3: Let it Go (Reclaiming Power)

As you can see, it actually takes some real work to get to this step. Once you notice and accept an emotion for what it is – an emotion – you have separated yourself from it. You are no longer in reaction mode. Instead, you have the ability to *respond*. You can respond by choosing to deny the emotion the opportunity to sabotage your day.

By completing the first two steps, your little one engages their prefrontal cortex, the part of the brain responsible for decision-making. This gives them the ability to respond to their environment instead of reacting with the "reptilian" part of their brain, which is responsible for basic survival impulses.

CPSIA information can be obtained
at www.ICGtesting.com
Printed in the USA
BVHW020655240721
612789BV00004B/7